THIS BOOK BELONGS TO
The Masked Avenger

THE AMBER AMULET

THE AMBER AMULET

by CRAIG SILVEY

ALLEN&UNWIN
SYDNEY•MELBOURNE•AUCKLAND•LONDON

Published by Allen & Unwin in 2012
Copyright © Craig Silvey 2012

Every effort has been made to contact the copyright holders of material
reproduced in this book. In cases where these efforts were unsuccessful,
the copyright holders are asked to contact the publisher directly.

Allen & Unwin
Sydney, Melbourne, Auckland, London
83 Alexander Street
Crows Nest NSW 2065
Australia
Phone: (61 2) 8425 0100
Fax: (61 2) 9906 2218
Email: info@allenandunwin.com
Web: www.allenandunwin.com

Cataloguing-in-Publication details are available from
the National Library of Australia
www.trove.nla.gov.au

ISBN 978 1 74237 998 2

Text and jacket design by Sandy Cull, gogoGingko
Jacket and internal illustrations by Sonia Martinez
Set in 12/15 pt Granjon by Bookhouse, Sydney
Printed in China, produced through Phoenix Offset

10 9 8 7 6 5 4 3 2 1

The Masked Avenger can make things happen.

Though at twelve he is considered young for a Justice Fighter, he has already proved himself highly effective in the pursuit of peace. His developing powers are so potent, so vast, that not even *he* can fully comprehend their extent. He has a number of astonishing abilities. For example, on certain occasions, he can summon a wall of cloud and make the sky roar. Then he'll point upwards and say *zap!* and sometimes a white vein of electricity will crackle loose and stab the earth. Other times he can sweep his arms and say *whoosh!* and the air will swoon at his command. When his powers are unfocused, he can only manage to shuffle dead leaves, but other times he can bend the spines of trees and make citizens huddle into their own arms. Soon, when he gains full control of his faculties, he'll be able to lash his enemies with gales and incinerate them with lightning.

The Masked Avenger derives his powers by harnessing the dormant energy that lies within objects that citizens overlook. He *believes* in energy. He's convinced the world is positively and negatively charged, that it's imbued with the properties of Good and Evil.

Energy is ubiquitous. It's present in sunlight, gravity, electricity, heat, food, movement. It's even inside the bodies of citizens, urgent and ready for release. But the world is also teeming with *trapped* energy, *potential* energy, buried beneath our feet and waiting to be unlocked. And nobody suspects, nobody understands its significance.

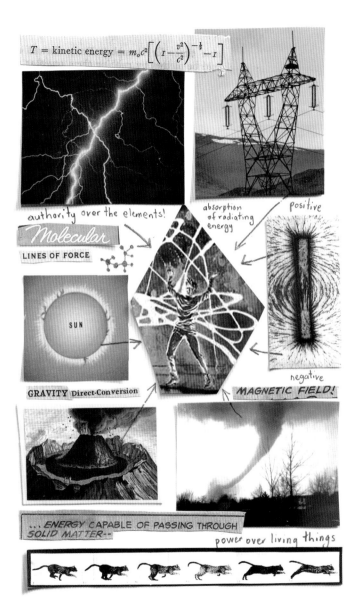

$$T = \text{kinetic energy} = m_o c^2 \left[\left(I - \frac{v^2}{c^2} \right)^{-\frac{1}{2}} - I \right]$$

authority over the elements!

Molecular

LINES OF FORCE

absorption of radiating energy

positive

SUN

GRAVITY Direct-Conversion

negative

MAGNETIC FIELD!

... *ENERGY CAPABLE OF PASSING THROUGH SOLID MATTER--*

power over living things

Except the Masked Avenger.

Only he knows that there's a secret ultra-concentrated energy in certain gemstones and minerals, and that they emit specific powers according to their molecular composition. These powers, when expertly applied, can be directly transferred into the body, resulting in superhuman capabilities.

Only the Masked Avenger has learnt to access the energy inside these gems and minerals and, as long as he is in contact with them, he alone is privy to their extraordinary power.

As such, his forest-green supersuit features a vital piece of equipment: his Amazing Powerbelt. It is a leather band of perfectly balanced geological items that neatly circum-navigates his waist. It features quartz, for Balance and Reason; jasper, for Intensity and Alertness; and a single tiger's eye, for unparalleled Speed and Agility. It also has one dollar eighty worth of coins, whose constituent nickel affords him a priceless amount of Strength

indetectable
to ordinary
citizens

CRYSTAL PRISMS
light wave refractions = INVISIBILITY?
QUARTZ

heartstone
honesty
truth,

amethyst

19 20 21

opposite forces ⟷
good ⟷ evil

concentrated
power

DIAMOND
Hardest known mineral. Crystallized deep down
at high temperature and pressure, and brought
to surface in ''kimberlite'' pipes. Photograph
shows a crystal in kimberlite. Most diamonds
are used in industry, for cutting or abrasive
purposes.   *Kimberley, South Africa*

COAL
Bituminous coal showing banded
structure.   *United Kingdom*

potential energy

and Endurance. Adhered is a small lump of granite, for Poise and Determination. And most importantly, four rough buttons of amethyst, for Truth and Honesty.

Adorning his wrist is a copper bracelet that his grandmother wore to soothe her arthritis, but he knows it is better used to amplify Empathy and Mercy. Pinned to his heart is his grandfather's bronze service medal, for Bravery and Valour. Two clear silicon discs secured in a wire frame rest on the bridge of his nose. They give his eyes Supersight, as well as protecting them against Debris, Hypnosis and Poking.

He also wears a red sheencape and a bandana mask hewn from the same material. These offer him the qualities of Defence and Anonymity.

His alloy of energy is almost impenetrable, but he does harbour vulnerabilities. If an enemy managed to somehow strip him of these accoutrements, he would lose his edge and need to rely purely on his own Cunning.

And there are other dangers.

Fortunately, it is not commonly known that black stones emit troubling amounts of dark energy. This makes them incredibly powerful, but also highly unpredictable and very dangerous. The Masked Avenger worries over these implications. So much so that he has personally written on a monogrammed sheet to the Prime Minister, warning him that if evildoers availed themselves of large amounts of sapphire, onyx, volcanic glass or meteorite, it would cause nothing short of a Global Cataclysmic Disaster. He also warned against the continued misuse of coal and oil, whose destructive nature has been well documented.

As yet, he has received no Official Reply. It may well point to a conspiracy.

In the end, the Masked Avenger knows it will be left to him to save the world. So he needs to improve his skill set by furthering his research in his secret lair. He needs to be stronger and better prepared. He wishes he had access to more precious materials so that he might unlock further superpowers, such as

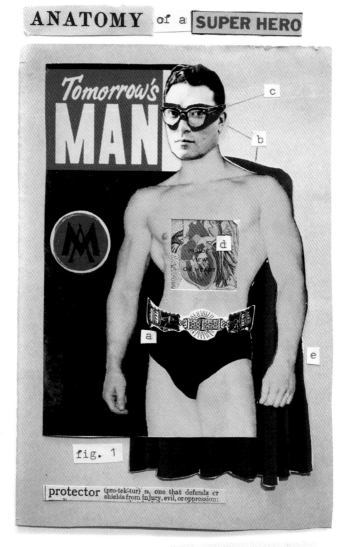

fig. 1

protector (pro-tek-tur) *n.* one that defends or shields from injury, evil, or oppression:

The MASKED AVENGER

a. POWERBELT

amethyst
truth
, honesty

quartz
balance
reason

granite
poise
determination

jasper
intensity
alertness

nickel
strength
endurance

tiger's eye
speed
agility

Flight, Lightspeed and Invulnerability. He has a suspicion that diamonds will be his key to defying gravity and that a plate of platinum might be his ticket to bulletproof skin. A collection of rubies, he anticipates, will give him ferocious Strength beyond the capabilities of any mortal creature. The application of mercury should offer him astonishing acceleration and a small bar of gold might well grant him telekinetic facilities.

And while he's clearly still refining his unique method of geo-alchemy, there is no denying his results so far. The Masked Avenger presides over a particularly peaceful neighbourhood. Franklin Street is clean, orderly and respectful. Everything here is in its right place, thanks in no small part to his discreetly vigilant watch.

He wishes it were possible, but he can't manage to patrol every night, a problem which led him to develop an ingenious solution: the Magnetometer. A little over a month ago, he carefully placed magnets near the doorways

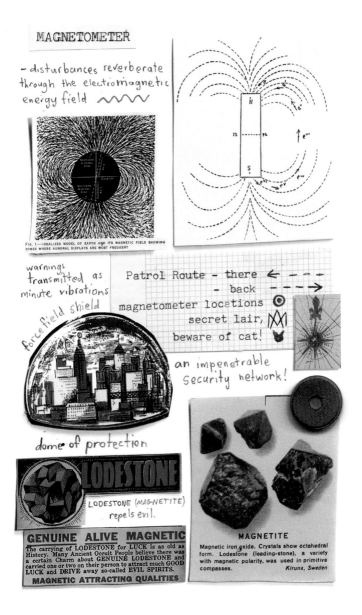

MAGNETOMETER

- disturbances reverberate through the electromagnetic energy field

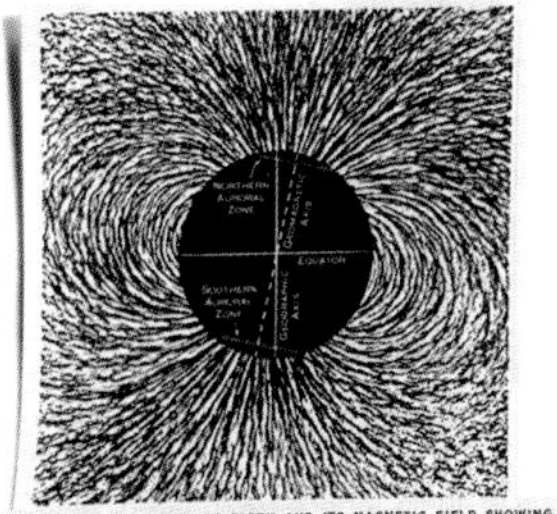

FIG. 1.—IDEALIZED MODEL OF EARTH AND ITS MAGNETIC FIELD SHOWING ZONES WHERE AURORAL DISPLAYS ARE MOST FREQUENT

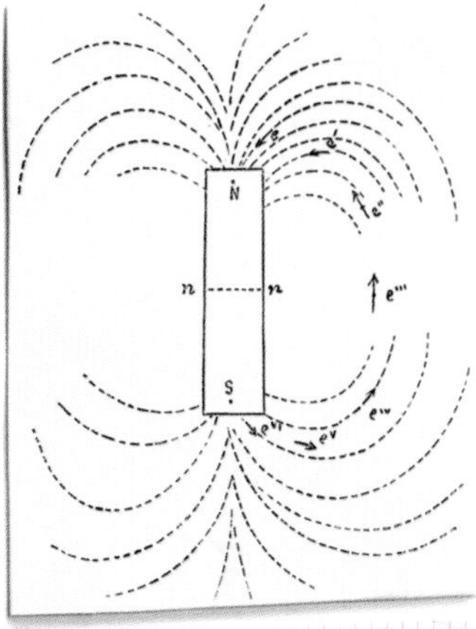

warnings transmitted as minute vibrations

Patrol Route - there ←---
- back --->
magnetometer locations
secret lair,
beware of cat!

forcefield shield

an impenetrable security network!

dome of protection

LODESTONE (MAGNETITE) repels evil.

MAGNETITE

Magnetic iron oxide. Crystals show octahedral form. Lodestone (leading-stone), a variety with magnetic polarity, was used in primitive compasses. *Kiruna, Sweden*

GENUINE ALIVE MAGNETIC

The carrying of LODESTONE for LUCK is as old as History. Many Ancient Occult People believe there was a certain Charm about GENUINE LODESTONE and carried one or two on their person to attract much GOOD LUCK and DRIVE away so-called EVIL SPIRITS.

MAGNETIC ATTRACTING QUALITIES

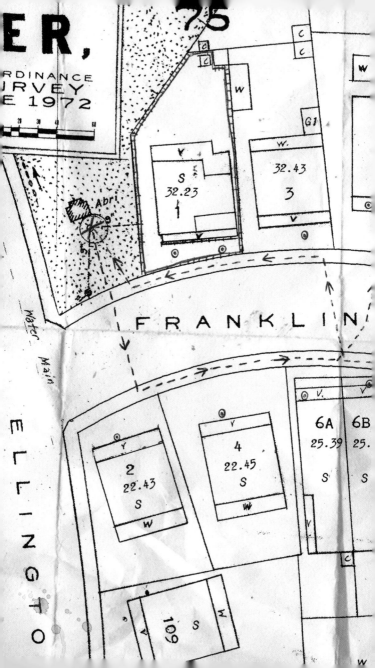

of every house on the street because magnets possess the powers of Connectivity and Communion. He keeps a disc of his own in the pocket of his supersuit, creating a satellite for disturbances and danger. Should he feel a strange hot hum at his thigh, he knows Trouble is afoot and somebody is in need of a Hero. It's a kind of extrasensory perception, the same way a dog can smell a tumour or a snake can see heat. The Masked Avenger knows when things are awry, when the balance between Good and Evil has shifted.

He is particularly concerned by the woman in the house at the end of the street. Something there is deeply amiss, though he can't quite put his finger on it. It's just a queasy feeling he gets. He has placed two magnets by her door, just to make sure she's safe.

*T*ONIGHT HE MAKES HIS patrol. Carefully he prises open the glass hatch of his secret lair and climbs outside.

He turns to assist the scrabbling emergence of his Partner in Justice, his loyal crime-fighting comrade, Richie the Powerbeagle, whose monogrammed tartan Thunderjacket boasts an aluminium foil insert to ward away dark energy.

They share a curiously strong interspecies bond. In fact, yet another superskill wielded by the Masked Avenger is an innate dominion over all fauna. He can instantly tame wild

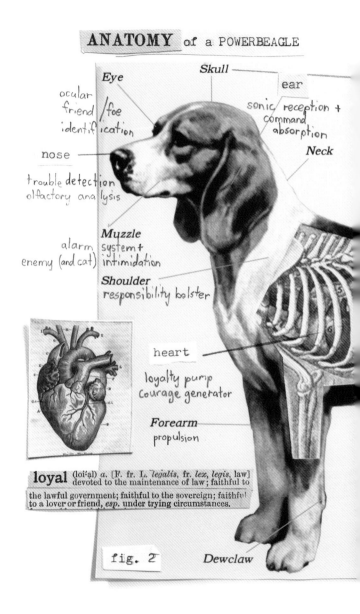

ANATOMY of a POWERBEAGLE

Skull

Eye

ear

ocular
friend /foe
identification

sonic reception +
command
absorption

Neck

nose

trouble detection
olfactory analysis

Muzzle
system +
intimidation

alarm
enemy (and cat)

Shoulder
responsibility bolster

heart

loyalty pump
Courage generator

Forearm
propulsion

loyal (loi'al) *a.* [F. fr. L. *legalis,* fr. *lex, legis,* law]
devoted to the maintenance of law; faithful to
the lawful government; faithful to the sovereign; faithful
to a lover or friend, *esp.* under trying circumstances.

fig. 2

Dewclaw

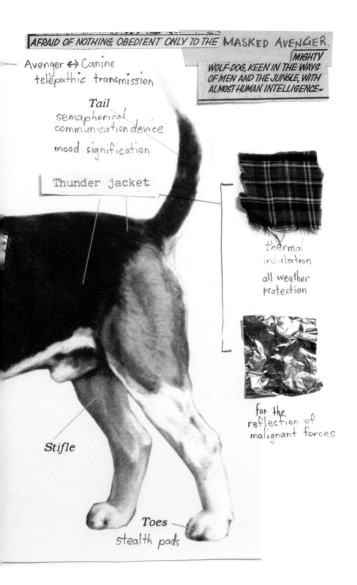

AFRAID OF NOTHING, OBEDIENT ONLY TO THE MASKED AVENGER

MIGHTY
WOLF-DOG, KEEN IN THE WAYS OF MEN AND THE JUNGLE, WITH ALMOST HUMAN INTELLIGENCE~

Avenger ↔ Canine
telepathic transmission

Tail
semaphorical
communication device

mood signification

Thunder jacket

thermal
insulation

all weather
protection

for the
reflection of
malignant forces

Stifle

Toes
stealth pads

animals and conduct their actions. For example, he can rush towards a cluster of ducks and command them to *fly!* and they will scatter like sparks and glide into the sky. He can creep up to a crouching cat and wave his hands and say *run!* and it will burst like a bullet.

His influence on Richie the Powerbeagle is even more profound. Incredibly, he can bid Richie to *sit!* or *lie down!* or *roll over!* or *stay there!* or *come here!* or any combination thereof, and it is immediately and obediently complied with.

The Masked Avenger never faces the unpredictable nature of The Street without Richie. Because, although they are dog and man, theirs is an infallible trust, a unique understanding that ensures their mutual protection and makes them formidable allies.

The fearless duo sneak to the back gate of the Compound of Justice.

'Sit, Richie,' instructs the Masked Avenger.

Richie sits. The gate swings open. They proceed.

The night is silent but he won't let that soften his focus. The Masked Avenger knows too well that Calm and Chaos share the same cold quiet. He stays loyal to the footpath, scanning for mayhem, scouring for deeds that need doing.

And look! Trouble already! The Wilsons have foolishly failed to present their bin for collection. Bidding Richie to sit, the Masked Avenger cocoons himself in his sheencape for Invisibility, and creeps towards the homestead. He deftly trundles the refuse vessel towards the kerb without alerting the security light. He nods once to his accomplice.

'Good job, Richie.'

They move on.

He crouches outside the house of Mrs Maud Fitzgerald, an elderly widow who's as grumpy as she is ungrateful. Not that her demeanour could sway his resolve. There appears to be a faulty hinge on her garden gate. He dips into his patented utility bag and removes his trusty pocket knife. A few tweaks on a few screws sets the gate straight and they continue their rounds.

Three houses down, a Volvo rests by the kerb with a slight slant. This can't be good. The Masked Avenger approaches carefully. Sure enough, the rear passenger tyre could do with some fresh air. He thumbs his chin.

'You know, Richie, I could probably inflate this with the strength of my own lungs but I'm not sure that will teach them the value of good car maintenance.'

Richie sits and looks up.

'You're right. We *have* to tell them. It's the only way they're going to learn.'

He kneels and removes a pen and a notepad from his utility bag. Very carefully he scribes his monogram at the head of the sheet, a broad M with the A piercing it like an arrow, cleverly creating a hidden diamond in the middle. Then he writes:

Dear Citizen,

Your back tyre is
dangerously low on
pressure. I would
suggest 36 psi for
safe driving.

Take Care,
The Masked Avenger

He secures the note and gives Richie a wink. They walk on. Near the end of the street, his Magnetometer begins to burn. He stops. Richie the Powerbeagle sniffs the air.

'You're right, Richie. It could be trouble.' He cocks his finger and thumb to look like a pistol, placing the barrel against his lips to quieten his comrade. Then he taps it forward, twice.

As usual, he identifies the house at the end of the street as the source of discontent, the one with two magnets and the woman he frets for. He approaches from the other side of the street, crouching behind a tree. From his utility pack, he removes his brass spyglass. He peers through it. There are lights on but no sounds.

He has listened and waited out here many times before. She's a striking woman, but elusive, with flame red hair and strong features. She doesn't look like she needs to be saved but the Masked Avenger knows different. From his limited investigations, he knows that she is married. Her husband is rarely home and, when he is, they often have loud rows and horrible quarrels. The nature of their arguments is always blurred by the walls.

The Masked Avenger has never intervened. Once he heard something smash, but before he could storm the premises her husband burst out the front door like an outlaw, kicked a potted plant and drove away fast. The woman stood on her doorstep and casually sucked a cigarette while his Magnetometer seared.

He thinks about her a great deal. He feels guilty for not having set things right. Tonight he wonders what he can do. He puts his hand on Richie's head and thinks hard. In a rush of import and confidence, having already neatly solved three dilemmas, he again pulls out his notepad.

He decides it's prudent to first make sure. If you're going to save a citizen pre-emptively, you'd best be confident your heroism is both necessary and required. He rests the pad on Richie's back. His first monogram is a little messy on account of his nerves. He strips it loose and tries again. Not bad. He taps the pen on his chin. Succinct is best. He writes.

M

IMPORTANT QUESTIONNAIRE

Are you unhappy?

☐ Yes
☐ No

(Please tick the appropriate box. It is important.)

Yours vigilantly,
The Masked Avenger

He folds, pauses, then slips across the street to post it in her letterbox.

'Come on, Richie,' he whispers. 'Let's head back.'

Once home, he will report to his Hero Log, citing his deeds done and adventures had.

And as they go, neither he nor Richie the Powerbeagle notice the curtain in the bay window slowly fall back into place.

URING THE DAY HE is mild-mannered
boy-genius Liam McKenzie. He carries
his secret close to his chest, not that
anybody would ever suspect him of moonlight
heroism. Though there are some boys in his
class he would love to show his powers to.

Still, in order to skirt any suspicion, occasionally he will be inconsistent in his behaviour.
He will be rude to his teacher, even though he
adores her and longs to disclose who he really is.
There are times when he will not submit homework that he has completed.

At home he will intermittently shirk his

chores or not eat his dinner, despite his intimate understanding of the value of Nutritional Energy. He will skirt the boundaries of Trouble and betray his virtues. He can sometimes be, as his mother says, Incredibly Unhelpful. Especially since he is now the Man of the House.

So far his red herrings have kept them off the scent. Nobody is aware of his superhuman capabilities or his services to the community. He's just a shy, whipsmart kid who slips up from time to time.

Thing is, Liam finds it harder to be a normal citizen than a Superhero. He navigates his nocturnal world with more comfort than his daily travails, which has led him to conclude that his *true* identity is the one he keeps hidden from view. That's the real secret of the vigilante: his face is his mask and his mask is his face. He *is* the Masked Avenger. Liam McKenzie is his act.

It's a burden he carries alone. Though on a certain level, of course, he knows that Richie understands. It must be hard for him too.

As soon as Liam is sent to bed, the Masked

Avenger climbs into his supersuit and secures his mask and sheencape with uncharacteristic haste. He gives Richie a fresh sheet of aluminium and straps him into his Thunderjacket.

It's dangerous to patrol on consecutive evenings but tonight he will accept the risk. It's still a long wait until the evening settles and most citizens are sleeping, so he slides the glass hatch and stares at the stars. He wonders what incredible minerals those galaxies have to offer. What he could do with a lump of moon rock! He could travel time or discover the secrets of the universe. He makes a mental note to draft a confidential letter to NASA.

Later, he walks the street with Richie. He notices with pride that the blue Volvo has inflated its tyres to the correct pressure. A note on the windscreen says: *Thank you!* He keeps it for his records.

Other than that, he takes in very little. His work is sloppy tonight, his attention compromised. He's distracted. In truth, he just wants to get to the house at the end of the street.

The lights are on but again it is quiet. There are no signs of activity or disorder, not even the spastic flicker of a television screen. His Magnetometer is curiously steady. He waits and scans. Then, carefully, he yawns open the letterbox, wincing as it creaks. He reaches in and takes the note. He can't bear to read it in the open.

In his hurry to leave, he drops the lid and it claps down loud. He ducks and holds his breath. Then he motions to Richie and they hastily exit.

In his secret lair he spreads the note under a lamp. His eyes widen. There it is. A single red tick that confirms his suspicions.

She is unhappy.

T HE MASKED AVENGER PACES restlessly into the night. In replying to his Important Questionnaire, she has entrusted him with her care. She is now his civic responsibility. He has inherited her unhappiness. Overturning it has become his duty.

But how? He bounces ideas off Richie, who listens intently but seems ultimately unimpressed. It's a difficult problem to solve without being privy to the origins of her complaint. For all his expertise in the fields of mineralogy and metallurgy, he can't be sure that there is a gem that cures unhappiness outright. He needs something far-reaching and proven. Something truly special.

He flicks through his geology books and pores over his set of rescued encyclopedias (he found them kerbside on one of his patrols). He draws diagrams on his blackboard, writes equations and notations only to erase them out of frustration.

Then he clicks his fingers.

He rushes to his desk. He prods the glossary of his official gemtome and quickly locates what he's looking for. He clears his blackboard with wide strokes and frantically calculates.

He's got it.

He whirls around to look at Richie, his cape following like hair in a shampoo advertisement.

'Richie!'

The Powerbeagle wakes up, looks alert.

'Richie, I've got it! It's so simple. *Amber!* We'll give her the Amber Amulet!'

THE AMBER AMULET, ON account of its precious properties, is fiercely guarded by a sleeping giant not far from his secret lair. Furthermore, it lies locked inside a barely penetrable chest, which may or may not feature an intricate security system.

It is a mission of immense bravery against inconceivable odds. The punitive measures for being caught don't bear thinking about. But it's a journey he must take. A woman's life is in his hands.

The Masked Avenger double-checks his Amazing Powerbelt and holds a series of acrobatic stretches. He removes his all-terrain powerboots and covers each foot with a cotton stealth-sheath. A Hero must be versatile.

He walks a tightrope down the hall. Slowly he pushes open the entrance to the sleeping giant's quarters. In the murky dimness, he makes out her figure, curled in the centre of the bed, breathing deep and heavy. Her chest rises and falls to a steady beat. For a mortally dangerous creature, she looks quite peaceful and beautiful. But he must not linger. Any false move could see her detonate.

He finds the chest that is home to the Amber Amulet on a nearby dresser. He stands before it and deftly manipulates the locking system. He incrementally lifts the lid. A sudden move here could be fatal. He locates the amulet easily and he takes it up with his breath held. Fortunately, no sirens blare. He has a lighter touch than he thought. He slips out of the room and closes the door.

On his way back to the secret lair, the Masked Avenger is interrupted by a scratching sound behind him. He wheels round. He has left Richie inside! His comrade is trapped! He must free him before it's too late!

He turns the knob and pushes but the door bangs Richie on the top of the head, which in the tense air issues the same report as a cannon in an empty gorge. Sure enough, the sleeping giant has been disturbed. She rustles and rises and quickly flaps at her bedside lamp. She spasms and gasps upon seeing him.

'*Liam?* Jesus Christ, you *scared* me!'

The Masked Avenger faces certain death!

'Sorry,' he wilts, trying to back out of the door.

'Wait! Come back here! What are you wearing? Is that your tracksuit? Why are you wearing a mask? Is that . . . that better not be my good silk slip that you've cut holes in. Why aren't you in bed?'

The Masked Avenger is in grave peril! All could unravel! Could this be the end?

'I . . . I just came in here to see if you were all right.'

She shakes her head but her frazzled frown softens. She sighs.

'You should be in bed, Liam. Not up and playing games with Richie.'

He nods. Could the Masked Avenger make it out unscathed?

'What time is it? Jesus, Liam, you've got school in a couple of hours. And I don't want you creeping around the house like this. It makes me feel the *opposite* of all right, do you understand? Go. To bed. Now!'

He is dismissed. Richie flees.

Back in his secret lair, he holds the amber up to the light. It's a rich glassy orb of burnished butterscotch. Trapped inside is the delicate husk of a tiny spider. It's beautiful. It's going to work too. It's going to save that woman.

It's too risky to deliver it tonight. He'll have to wait it out and lie low.

For now, he conceals the Amber Amulet under his pillow and gives Richie a chicken-flavoured energy unit. He rubs his tender head and apologises for putting him in danger.

fig. 9

'I came back for you though, Richie. Remember that.'

With hope in his heart, the Masked Avenger reports to his Hero Log, disrobes and retires for the evening.

H E WAITS TWO LONG DAYS before he suits up again, which allows him time to work on his response. To further protect his identity, he carts in an old typewriter.

He sweats over the reply, tapping out dozens of drafts. A Hero must be concise but detailed. He must be warm but authoritative. It's a difficult balance to strike.

Finally, he ends up with a memorandum both he and Richie are happy with.

He secures the amulet to the page with its own pin. Then he tucks the letter into an envelope that features his finest official monogram

M

Dear Ma'am,

Thank you for answering my Important
Questionnaire. I don't mean to pry,
but saving people is my calling.

Please find enclosed this AMBER AMULET.
It will protect you from sadness.

That must sound unusual to a citizen,
but you will have to trust me on this
count because the science is too detailed
for me to outline here.

All you need to know is that the AMBER
AMULET will eliminate your unhappiness
by counteracting it with POSITIVE ENERGY.

In order for it to work, you must wear
it at ALL times, ESPECIALLY when you
sleep, because that's where sadness
gains strength.

If you follow my directions, this should
see you straight. Just to be sure, I
have taken the liberty of installing a
MAGNETOMETER in front of your home, so I
know instantaneously if you're ever in
need of my help.

Fear not, you're in safe hands now.

Take care,

The Masked Avenger

The Masked Avenger

(it's important she knows this isn't the work of an impostor).

He also makes a separate copy for his Hero Log.

On his way to her house he notices a garden sprinkler is not performing optimally. His preliminary assessment leans towards a congested filter. He vows to clear it out on the way back.

He also shifts a stranded bicycle that was outside its property line closer to its carport, because villains love an easy target.

He arrives. There are no lights on. Perhaps she's taking an early night or she's out. He takes a quick scan through his spyglass before deciding to leave the envelope. Then he walks into the adjacent park and sits on a swing set in the shadows, waiting to see if she emerges. She doesn't.

He heads for his secret lair by way of the faulty sprinkler.

THREE DAYS LATER LIAM McKenzie arrives home from school and sees his mother in distress. She looks dishevelled and her eyes are pink and puffy. He slowly drops his bag.

'What's wrong?'

She runs a hand through her hair.

'Liam, I need to talk to you. Come and sit down.'

Liam sits down. Richie trots out of the room.

'Listen. I am missing something *very* precious. Do you have any idea what that might be?'

She searches his widening eyes. Liam

McKenzie must again skirt the border of Trouble and betray his principles.

He shrugs and shakes his head. His mother exhales and rubs her cheeks with both hands. She looks very tired.

'I'm missing an amber brooch from my jewellery box. Are you sure you haven't seen it or touched it? It's okay, you're not in any trouble if you have, I just want to know if you've moved it, that's all.'

Liam's bottom lip blooms. He shakes his head again.

'No,' he clears his throat. 'No, I definitely haven't seen it. I'm sorry.'

'Really? Oh, God. I was *really* hoping you knew where it was. I can't understand where it is. It's just . . . missing. From out of my jewellery box. I haven't worn it in years but I see it there every day. It was my grandmother's brooch, Liam, and it is very, *very* important to me. If it's gone . . .'

His mother's eyes get glassy and her voice gets thick.

'We'll find it,' says Liam. 'We'll look every-where.'

'I *have* looked everywhere. But it doesn't make sense for it to be somewhere other than that box. I don't understand. It *must* have been stolen. It's the only answer. Maybe it was the plumber who was here last week. But if it *has* been stolen, why just that brooch? Why not anything else?'

'You're right,' says Liam, who has a sick cold weight in his stomach. 'It doesn't add up.'

'It's all I had left of her, and it was her favourite thing in the world. She wore it every-where. I can't believe I've lost it. I will never forgive myself. I *have* to find it. It can't be gone.'

She gets up, distracted. Then she sits back down again.

'I'm sorry,' says Liam with a lump in his throat. And he means it.

'It's okay,' she sighs. 'It's not your fault.'

*T*HAT NIGHT THE MASKED Avenger very slowly suits up. His mask is a limp ribbon in his hands. He takes a deep breath.

In trying to enact one Right, he has invited a whole cluster of Wrongs. He has tried to cure a citizen's unhappiness with a potent piece of amber but its absence from its rightful place has caused untold misery.

The Masked Avenger has his work cut out. This is his sternest test, his hour of reckoning. It will test his loyalty, his courage and his mettle. He has no choice: he must retrieve the Amber Amulet!

But how? He can't simply ask for it. A Hero can't develop trust with troubled citizens by admitting mistakes and meekly retracting life-altering items. It would be humiliating. And besides, this woman *believes* in him, she has enlisted his expertise! If she suspects him of being a fraud, she could spiral into a cesspool of dejection!

He paces.

He clicks his fingers. Maybe it's still in her letterbox! It's only been three days, she may not have checked her mail. He has a faint flutter of hope in his chest. He has to go there. Tonight.

But if she *has* taken the amulet? What then? He will have to employ desperate measures. There is only one way. He will need to infiltrate the premises and steal it back.

It's a serious mission. He'll need to be on top of his game. Because he knows precisely where the amulet will be: pinned to her chest, just as he instructed.

Stealth will be critical. He'll need a cool hand and an iron will. He can't afford schoolboy errors like his last excursion. He can't be locking his comrade inside the arena of danger. He'll need to be clean and sharp. Professional.

For the first time as a Superhero, he is suddenly arrested by volts of nerves. Maybe he *should* just request its return, to hell with the loss of face. After all, it's only one citizen in a metropolis of many. Or even just let the amulet go, forget it ever happened. His mother will mend.

But down the hall, he can hear her restless rustling, turning things over, shifting furniture, riffling drawers. He clenches his grandfather's service medal and closes his eyes, feeling its power coursing through his bloodstream.

He is ready.

But before he leaves, he uses a penknife to pick away the four shards of amethyst from his Amazing Powerbelt. A Hero must never betray his attributes. He drops them in a drawer and promises to earn them back.

⚡

a. POWERBELT

~~amethyst~~
~~truth~~
~~honesty~~

quartz
balance
reason

granite
poise
determination

jasper
intensity
alertness

nickel
strength
endurance

tiger's eye
speed
agility

BEING A STATE OF EMERGENCY, the Masked Avenger doesn't bother to patrol. He glides down the footpath towards her house and observes. The lights are off. A good sign.

He and Richie sneak over. Holding his breath, he lifts the lid of her letterbox. It is empty.

He sits on the pavement, shielded by a hedge. His head rolls back. The Masked Avenger accepts his fate. He has to go in.

The front of her house is too exposed. Any number of neighbours could witness his trespass. He decides to course up the flank of the adjoining park and enter from the back. It's a classic tactical manoeuvre. From the rear, he'll have the time and safety he needs to find an impromptu entrance. He can wriggle a window, squeeze through a catflap, work the lock with his knife. He'll have to play it by ear.

'Come on, Richie. It's time. We have to do this.'

They sneak, quickly and quietly, following a high pine picket fence, which is garlanded by a thin vine. His heightened senses detect citronella and tobacco in the air. He can see easily through the gaps in the fence. He extends his spyglass and peers. A floodlight spreads across the woman's backyard, and there she is, sitting on her back porch with a cigarette and a novel. He thinks he can see the amulet on her left collarbone. He looks for entrances and options.

It's impossible! *Impenetrable!* There must be another way. Attempting the operation now would be a suicide mission. He snaps his spyglass shut and looks down to think. His temple pounds. This is harder than he thought. He can't blaze his way to victory right now. He needs a more intricate scheme. He should head back to his secret lair to develop an infallible plan.

'Come on, Richie. Let's go.'

He looks to his left but Richie is not there. He swivels and scans the park but he can't locate his partner. Confused, he peers back through the fence into her yard and that's where he sees Richie. Squatting. Bashfully taking a shit on her lawn.

The Masked Avenger gasps. What is he *doing*? Is this cold betrayal or a misguided attempt at a diversion? Either way, it makes little sense. He has to get him out of there.

'*Richie!*' he hisses, '*Richie!*'

But his comrade doesn't hear or understand. His powers of Interspecies Communion seem to be ebbing.

He glances toward the porch. The woman hasn't looked up from her book. There's still a chance they might make it out.

Richie has finished his business and is now inspecting the property with his nose. How has she not seen him?

'*Richie!*' he hisses a little louder. 'Richie, come *here!*'

The woman looks up and directly at the fence. He lurches backwards and the impact has him sitting on something sharp in his utility belt. He cries out in shock and pain.

Now the woman stands up and squints in his direction. Then she frowns at Richie the Powerbeagle.

'Who's there?'

He panics and says nothing. Through the fence he can see that Richie is also looking his way. This is not his finest hour. Still, he can't leave him there. He's just laid a turd on her lawn. She might call the ranger to have him executed. He clears his throat.

'It's me, ma'am. The Masked Avenger.'

'Oh.'

'I'm sorry,' he quickly adds. 'I was just making sure you were safe. And I'm sorry about . . . my accomplice. I can clear that up.'

'That's no problem,' she calls out. 'Why don't you come over so we can talk properly?'

He breathes heavily and looks around.

'I can't, ma'am.'

'Why not?'

'It might compromise my identity.'

She pauses.

'But don't you have a mask?'

Silence. He's stuck! She's smarter than he thought.

'Okay,' he offers eventually.

He glances at the gap under the fence that Richie crawled through. No chance. He'll have to go over.

The Masked Avenger takes a running start, leaps and hoists himself over the fence. The pickets are sharper than he'd imagined, so he hurries his dismount and lands messily. However, he's spared a spectacular tumble by his cape, which has snagged itself on a picket and suspended him at an awkward angle. He flails his arms to no avail. The woman crosses the lawn to unhook him. She smells nice. He looks up from the Amber Amulet and sees that she has a bruised eye. He looks down.

'Thank you,' he says, and arranges his sheencape.

'Come sit down,' she urges and waves.

'Oh, you know, I shouldn't stay. I'll just collect my partner and get going.'

'Come on,' she smiles warmly. 'We should talk. It's okay.'

She wears a quizzical smile, as though she finds him somehow faintly amusing. Perhaps it's testament to the effectiveness of the amulet. She's deliriously happy under its spell, narcotically content. Nevertheless, the Masked Avenger senses the balance between Hero and Citizen has shifted. He clicks into gear and looks up.

'Would you like to sit down, ma'am?' he asks, his arm gesturing towards the porch. 'We should probably talk. I'd be interested to see how you're doing.'

Her brow furrows slightly but she agrees. She is very pretty, with untied hair and creamy skin and a generous smile. They sit under the porch.

'Would you like a drink?' she asks.

'No, thank you. I can't accept gifts.'

'I see. My name is Joan, by the way.'

He nods. Richie slumps heavily by his feet and exhales. Again he feels his authority slipping, so he asks a question.

'Do you know what amber is, Joan?'

He adds her name as an afterthought, thinking it will make him sound a little more professorial and wise.

She unlatches the amulet and holds it in her lap.

'Not really, no.'

'It's a fossil. Made out of tree resin.'

'Is that so?'

'It is. It takes at *least* ten million years to make amber. Ten *million* years, sitting there under the earth. Then most of it washes up by the Baltic Sea. People collect it. Do you know where the Baltic Sea is?'

'I do, yes.'

'It's in Europe.'

'It is.'

'So you've got this fossil being formed over millions of years, under *incredible* pressure and heat, and the whole time it's collecting energy. That's why it's so potent. The same as other gems and metals and rocks, which take just as long to make. But amber is different because it's made of resin, which is like a plant's blood. It helps to heal the tree. And that's why people, ages ago, thought that amber could heal *them*. They used it as medicine, for sore throats and things. But I know different.'

'How so?'

'Because it's full of ultra-concentrated positive energy, enough for more than your lifetime. And just by touching it, you can transfer it into your body on a molecular level. The Amber Amulet is kind of miraculous when you think about it. Millions and millions of years ago, in *Europe*, it oozed out of a tree and that little spider got stuck in it, then it got buried underground, then it was put in a basket, then a boat, then it was brought over here and then given to you.'

'That's really something.'

He's clearly impressed her with his expertise. And her enthusiasm goads him on, the words bubble out of his mouth. He perches on the edge of his chair.

'See, *everything* has energy. Think about it. Coal, for example. It's just fossilised trees and we turn it into electricity. Same as petrol, which is just really old bits of fish, and the world runs on it! So it makes sense that something like amber, and other stones and metals, are full of different kinds of energies because they're made of different stuff. The secret is how to unlock them. They did it with the atom, remember? They chopped one up, and look how much energy came out. A thing that tiny, it blew up a city!'

'It certainly did.'

'Energy is everywhere, Joan. And energy is power. If you can harness more energy, you become powerful.'

THE ATOM

URANIUM ORE

dark materials

energy (en'er-ji) *n.* [G. *en*, in, and *ergon*, work] in-ternal or inherent power ; power efficiently and forcibly exerted; effectual operation; efficacy; strength of expression ; emphasis ; capacity for performing work or moving against resistance ; vigour ; strength ; spirit ; efficiency.

'Like you.'

'Well, I'm still learning, really. Unfortunately, my gem collection is quite limited but I'm building it up. When I get better materials like diamonds and rubies and gold, I'll have more impressive powers and I'll be able to save more people. I'm working on telekinesis at the moment. That's when you can move objects with your mind, because energy can move through the air. That's what Nikola Tesla discovered. He was a genius. He worked out that every second, all over the world, there are a hundred bolts of lightning. And he wanted to get access to all that energy but he couldn't work out how. Did you know that a lightning bolt is hotter than the sun, Joan?'

'No I did not.'

'It is. But that's the thing. There is *so* much energy around us and we don't know how to use it properly. It gets wasted. That's why there are so many fat people. They take in so much energy but they don't use it and so it just sits there. That's what fat is. It's energy that doesn't

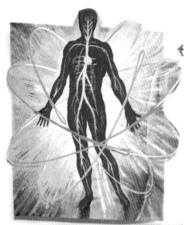

Additional minerals necessary to release trapped energy and achieve *full potential*

DIAMOND, RUBY, ~~ONYX~~ PLATINUM, MERCURY, OPAL SILVER? GOLD...

At depths below those of the present deepest mine, we may one day find new minerals that are stable at the high pressures and temperatures nearer the centre of the Earth. The advent of space travel opens up the possibility of the discovery of new minerals which would be stable on other planets where conditions are so different from our own.

▼ harnessing electrical energy

REPUBLIKA HRVATSKA

250

Nikola Tesla

"man-made lightning"

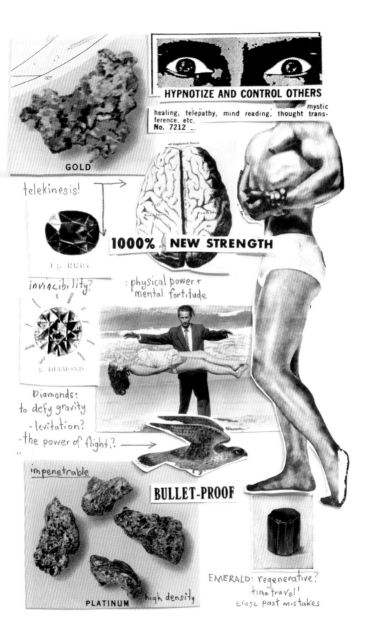

GOLD

HYPNOTIZE and CONTROL OTHERS

healing, telepathy, mind reading, thought transference, etc.
No. 7212

mystic

telekinesis!

1000% NEW STRENGTH

1 3. RUBY

invincibility?

3. DIAMOND

: physical power +
mental fortitude

Diamonds:
to defy gravity
- levitation?
- the power of flight?

impenetrable

BULLET-PROOF

PLATINUM   high density

EMERALD: regenerative?
time travel!
erase past mistakes

get used up. It's *potential* energy. Same as fossils and gems and metals. And humans. It's all just energy waiting to happen.'

She suddenly rears back at this, flinching like he's just struck at her unexpectedly. That giddy smile is gone and she stares at him in a way that makes him slightly uneasy. He supposes she must be in awe. Her eyes are wide. Probably with wonder. She is marvelling. Because he is marvellous.

'Anyway,' he smoothes his sheencape, 'that's all a secret. I've never told anyone all of that before.'

'It's okay. I won't tell.'

'I hope not, Joan. If my enemies came to know this, it could be a monumental calamity.'

'You can trust me. I promise. But how about I give you a secret in return? That way you'll have one on me if I tell.'

'That's fair,' he nods.

'Well,' she holds her hands up for a moment and drops them on her thighs. 'What would you like to know?'

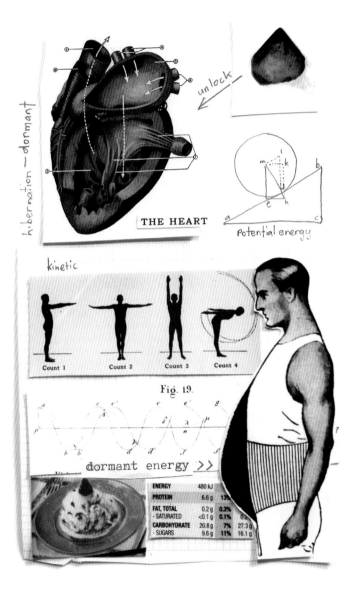

hibernation — dormant

unlock

THE HEART

potential energy

kinetic

Count 1 Count 2 Count 3 Count 4

Fig. 19.

dormant energy >>

ENERGY	480 kJ		
PROTEIN	6.6 g	13%	
FAT, TOTAL	0.2 g	0.3%	
- SATURATED	<0.1 g	0.1%	
CARBOHYDRATE	20.8 g	7%	27.3 g
- SUGARS	9.6 g	11%	16.1 g

The Masked Avenger pauses for a moment. Then he points a finger at his eye.

'How did I get my black eye?' she asks.

He nods once.

'Actually,' she sighs, 'the truth is very embarrassing. I popped a champagne cork into my eye. Can you believe it? It was terrible. It was at a lunch event at my work. And the worst thing is that my boss was struggling to loosen the cork, so I snatched it off him. But I couldn't open it either and, bear in mind I was a little bit tipsy by this point, because I *actually* brought the bottle up to my face to inspect it, like I was looking through a telescope. And then *pow!* Out came the cork, right into my eye. I shot myself in the face trying to be the hero. It was the most profoundly stupid thing I have ever done in my life.'

The Masked Avenger can't help it, his nose twitches trying to stifle his smile but it spreads anyway.

'I'm sorry,' he says, and giggles. She smiles too.

'Hey, it's not funny! It really hurt! So here I was, staggering backwards because I'd just been *shot in the eye*, and I was *covered* in champagne, and the most humiliating thing is that the shock of it all made me cry. I started sobbing in front of all my colleagues. It was horrible. And now I have a black eye.'

'Oh no! I'm sorry. I shouldn't have laughed. That was unprofessional.'

'It was but I'll forgive you. You're not the first. Anyway, that's *my* secret.'

'I won't tell,' promises the Masked Avenger, who then quietly adds, 'I thought . . .'

'It was my husband?'

He nods.

'You and everyone else on this street, most likely. But I understand. We don't do ourselves any favours. But no. He would never, *ever* hit me.' She knits her brow and shakes her head quickly, as though the notion is absurd to her.

Joan looks out across the lawn.

'We do argue a lot but it's just . . .' she pauses again, fumbling for words. 'Frustration. Fear, maybe. I think we both realise that, you know . . . but we're both too terrified to do anything about it, and so yelling at each other and feeling miserable seem easier.'

She trails off and absently lights a cigarette. When she emerges from her thoughts, she smiles and shakes her head.

'Why on earth am I telling you all this?'

The Masked Avenger shrugs. After a time, he says, 'Maybe you both fell out of love.'

She tilts her head to the side, the same way Richie does when he doesn't understand a command.

'That's an interesting way to put it.'

'That's what happened to my parents. Well, it's how my mum explained it. They fell out of love. When I was really young, my dad just left without telling anybody but she tracked him down. He sees me every other weekend but I can tell his heart's not really in it. He has a whole other family and everything. Maybe he fell out of love with me too.'

'I don't think that's true.'

'You don't really know him.'

'That's true. I'm sorry.'

'So why *did* you love your husband?'

Joan inhales a deep awkward breath with her eyebrows high. She thinks.

'That's hard. I think in the beginning it was because he loved me, so I loved him back because I was grateful. I didn't like myself much back then and so I was attracted to the fact that he saw something in me worth loving. It's a real thrill being loved by someone who doesn't have to do it. And so I think I got married because I thought that a ring would lock that love in forever, because it's very scary when it is just your feelings holding you together.'

'So how come people fall out of love, do you think?'

'I don't know. It's true that people change. Or people *don't* change when you'd hoped they might. Or they find somebody else they like better. Or people just grow apart, they lose interest in each other's lives. Maybe they realise they made a mistake. There are lots of reasons.'

'What's yours?'

Joan laughs softly and shakes her head. She should scold him for his impertinence, maybe even send him home. But this strange boy is so genuine and innocently direct that it pins her. And something about that mask and uniform makes it all right, gives this the air of a confessional. She's suddenly hearing the questions she's routinely avoided for years and it stuns her. *No. Sit here and face it,* she thinks. *This is what you deserve.*

'Well, I'm not sure. The problem is, I got what I thought I wanted. I locked it all in by getting married, and now we both just feel trapped, like this little spider in the amber. But I always worked so hard to keep it going anyway because I thought that having someone to love, having someone love me back, made me a stronger person. But it was the opposite. It made me *weaker* because it led me to believe that I couldn't survive without those things. And I spent so long afraid of being alone that I never did anything for myself. I never did anything *with* myself, which made it all the easier to believe I wasn't capable. God, I don't know. Somewhere along the line we just stopped being *kind* to each other. I think most of the time when I'm yelling at my husband, I'm just yelling at myself.'

Joan is picking at the amulet and talking into her lap. The Masked Avenger isn't particularly clear on her testimony but he thinks he knows what to do. He unclasps his grandfather's service medal.

'If you need courage, I can give you this. It's bronze, which has incredibly strong properties. You just have to wear it, same as the amber.'

'You really would give that to me, wouldn't you?'

He shrugs and nods.

'Sacrifice, Joan. That's what makes a Hero.'

'Maybe it's better you keep it. But thank you. It's very kind.'

Her smile looks sad. He frowns. Her constant fiddling with the amber must have interrupted its flow of energy. He still has no idea how to get it back. He can't ask for it now, not with the way her shoulders have fallen forward. He's in a tight bind.

'You must be tired,' says Joan.

'Actually, I don't sleep all that much. Nikola Tesla had the same problem.'

'Too much energy?' she smiles.

'Something like that. I can't really switch off my brain like other people can because I have access to all the bits that normal citizens don't use. But that's all right. It works out fine. I mostly save people nocturnally anyway.'

The quiet descends. The Masked Avenger chews his lip and wracks his brain for a last ditch opportunity to wrest back control of the Amber Amulet. He desperately tries to summon the powers of telekinesis. No good. He closes his eyes and tries to conjure a storm, a hurricane, a bolt of lightning through the roof of this house. *Zap! Whoosh!*

Nothing works.

They sit for a long while until Joan turns with her eyebrows high.

'Well, *I* might call it a night. It's very late.'

'I should go,' he cuts in. Richie is dolefully slow to rise. The Masked Avenger lingers slightly, seeing the amulet in her hand.

'Joan?'

'Yes?'

He shakes his head quickly.

'It's okay.'

They walk through the house. The Masked Avenger pays careful attention, lest he needs to break in later. She opens the front door.

'It was nice talking to you, Joan. Things will be all right. You'll be happy again soon. You can believe in me.'

The Masked Avenger isn't sure how reassuring that was because she looks as though she might cry.

'You want to know another secret?' she asks.

'Sure.'

'I didn't realise how unhappy I was until you asked. Thank you for listening.'

The Masked Avenger isn't sure what to say, so he nods once and moves on. Richie trots alongside. Joan lights a cigarette as he trudges towards the front gate.

He turns quickly, snapping his fingers.

'Try rubbing an emerald around your eye. It should take care of the pain and the swelling.'

'All right. I will do that.'

'Goodnight, Joan,' he salutes.

'Goodnight,' she smiles and waves.

She leans against the architrave and wonders what just happened, and why her eyes are glazing. Her bruised socket feels hot and tender. *Emerald!* She smiles. And she recalls that moment when he had her rearing back and opening up: that one clear sentence amidst his beautiful admirable nonsense that had perfectly described the restlessness she'd felt all her life.

The Masked Avenger clips home, scolding himself for his predicament. He climbs inside his secret lair a failure, a charlatan. He has returned without the amulet. He is in deep trouble. He thinks about Joan, about the way she looked at the amber in her lap as she spoke, and knows he could never summon the insensitivity to ask for it back or even muster the temerity to deceitfully reacquire it. But that, in turn, leaves him severely in his mother's debt. He stole her heirloom and gave it away. He sits on his bed and rubs Richie's head.

'Richie, I think I shot myself in the face trying to be the Hero.'

The Masked Avenger looks at his reference books, his blackboard, his desk. He takes in the stack of pre-monogrammed pages next to his typewriter. He thinks about the amethyst buried in his drawer right next to his Hero Log. And with a curdling jolt of dread, he understands what he has to do.

*T*WO DAYS LATER, AS dawn creeps in, Liam McKenzie walks to his own letterbox on behalf of the Masked Avenger. There is dew on the lawn, and all is quiet, save for the occasional magpie warble. He surveys his peaceful street with a sad pride. He has plans. Big plans. One day he hopes to strike the right combination of precious materials to allow him to emit enough energy to project a giant force-field, an enormous invisible shell that repels all Evil and traps tranquillity. Everyone in its shade will be protected and safe, and he'll be able to walk the streets as their silent guardian.

But all of that is imperilled by the letter he's about to deliver. It's a full confession and unconditional apology made out to the rightful owner of the Amber Amulet.

He hopes she might understand the reason behind its disappearance, maybe find some solace in the fact that it was all in aid of a citizen in need. The letter asks for her forgiveness but understands why it might be withheld.

He knows it is likely he will be forced into retirement, or at the very least a protracted hiatus. During which time he can only imagine what kind of Evil might emerge from the shadows, emboldened by his absence.

He knows that leaving this letter is like throwing a grenade and running after it but he has no choice. In his left fist he grips a piece of amethyst, hoping it will guide him towards the right course of action. He takes a deep breath and lifts the tin flap.

That breath remains buried, because the letterbox reveals a bulky envelope addressed to the Masked Avenger. He glances around the street, then carefully pinches it out. His heart skips, and nearly bursts through his chest when he feels a small lump hidden inside the package. Still, a Hero needs to be careful. It could be a bomb. A ruse. A trap.

He bolts back to the secret lair and strips it open. Two very precious items fall free.

And there is a letter:

Dear Masked Avenger,

I just wanted to say thank you and goodbye, because I've decided to move away. I also wanted to return your very beautiful amulet.

As it turns out, I don't think a lack of good energy has been my problem. For a long time, I've been just like that amber you described – trapped underground, squeezed under pressure, and full of energy waiting to happen. I've certainly got enough to fill my lifetime, and I'm going to start using it.

However, I am going to keep using your magnetometer. I found it by my door, and if you don't mind, I'd like to keep it with me so you know I am doing well.

I think you are a truly remarkable hero. And somewhere along the line I lost all those wonderful things you have in spades. I hope you keep them close to your chest and guard them fiercely.

A strange thing about getting older is that you start telling yourself little lies to smooth over all the awkward things you'd rather not think about, or to cope with the things you can't change. You tell yourself 'It's alright' or 'I'm happy', and if you say it often enough, you start to believe it.

Sometimes all it takes is somebody to make you look at what you've been avoiding. And even though you know the truth already, it can be a real shock. It can feel as though you're looking at it for the very first time.

I don't imagine this makes a lick of sense to you, but I wanted to thank you for being so kind to a stranger. I think you have a terrific future as a hero ahead of you.

Take care,

Your friend,

Joan x

PS: You'll notice I have given you something for your collection. I couldn't think of a better home for it. I'm excited to think of all the new powers you'll find. I hope it serves you well.

Liam McKenzie wipes his eyes and nose and holds the amulet. His whole body feels slack and loose. He could collapse and spreadeagle and grin, he's so happy. He grabs Richie by the cheeks and nuzzles him so passionately his glasses come loose. Of course! It wasn't amber she needed, it was amethyst all along!

Shaking, he holds that honey-brown amulet up to the morning sun and its trapped spider sparkles like the diamond on the ring he's just been given.

fig. 12

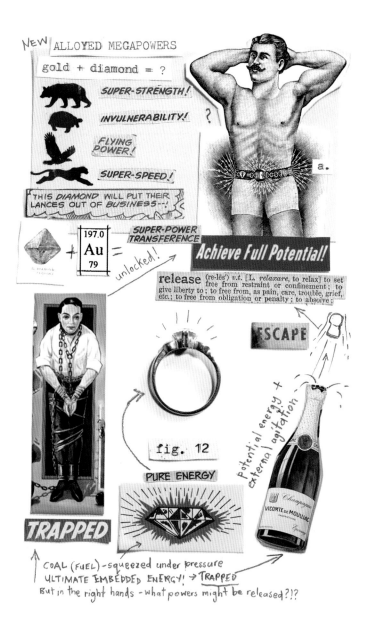